Shooting Stars & Written Hearts

KAASHVI BHARTIYA

BlueRose ONE .com
Stories Matter
New Delhi • London

BLUEROSE PUBLISHERS
India | U.K.

BlueRose ONE.com
Stories Matter
NewDelhi • London

For permissions requests or inquiries regarding this publication, please contact:

BLUEROSE PUBLISHERS
www.BlueRoseONE.com
info@bluerosepublishers.com
+91 8882 898 898
+4407342408967

ISBN: 978-93-6261-002-7

Cover design: Tahira
Typesetting: Tanya Raj Upadhyay

First Edition: June 2024

Acknowledgement

Thanks to my teacher who saw the light behind my words. Thanks to mom, who stood by me when everything else seemed hollow. To Nani, who showered her blessing in every step of my way. To my sister, who has always been my inspiration. To my brother, who is in fact my best friend. To dad, who pushed me forward. To my dog, who licks off all my face cream. Thanks to everyone who cheered the loudest, even when I stuttered.

My biggest thanks to everyone who entered my life and left with a lesson

To Mom,

whose strength becomes my shield.

Prologue

And that's the moment I realized - it all came down. My planets crashed into each other; I could see the stars falling in the form of tears. As I brought my knees up to my chest, covering my face with my hands, I felt myself surrounded by the warmth of a hug. I lifted my face, seeing him with stars falling down his face. I sank deeper into his arms trying to recall every memory, count every hug and 'love you' or promise to come every 3 months but still manage to plan a trip once every 365 days. It might be the only time I ever saw my brother cry. I didn't want to think about her but all I was wondering was, who will talk to mom every day, providing her the assurance of everything turning out to be right. Who will make sure I eat triple of my capability. Who will sit on that couch, the one she always sat on, there was no other place I would expect her to be. Nani!! (grandma). All I could do is wish to reach faster, mom needs me, I need to be there for her.

As I reached, climbing the stairs, just trying my best to do what's right. Repeating "I got to be there for her " under my breath. As I reached the last step, I was numb. The air. It was empty, like. Like someone took out all the shiny objects away from the world. Her absence was heart thrashing. I didn't want to believe that, actually I couldn’t. Not one cell in my body agreed to it.

As I walked down the hall and through the open archway, into the living room, there my mom. She seemed tensed, more like pale.

They are my family. Then why does their eyes strike under my skin making me question my every step, every move.

Now that She's not here, the place feels hollow. However, she's looking through that picture of hers. Her rooms are still called by her names, she's still here, everyone wants to believe it, so they are messing with reality, but reality doesn't like to be messed with, it will strike. When it does, they all will know. The deepening of breaths is not helping either. When I feel like I'm getting to places ...... The wall crashes down, I hate it all,

The breaths and the tears.

The stress and the anxiety.

If they are my family then why is it so hard to speak Infront of them.

If this is my home then why is there no warmth inside.

It's much more complicated than this.

My love for them is beyond compare but sometimes I feel that love's striking back, like no matter how hard I try, I going to fail

SIA

One

As I dug into my bag in search of a hair chip, the chaotic array of items within seemed to mock my efforts. A familiar voice echoed through the hallway, interrupting my quest. It was my mom, as she pulled me from my task, as I went over, I could already imagine the day ahead with my hair untamed.

"Yes mom "

Casting a curious glance at the wooden box that sat beside her. Pretty similar to the one my late grandma had in her room. Wait! I could find a rubber band in Grandma's room.

As land beside mom -

"Though physically absent, here lies a piece of your grandma she left for you ". Her words suddenly sent a surge of conflicting emotions coursing through me.

What!

With trembling hands I accepted the box, practically on the urge to drop it due to the nervousness and excitement running through me "excuse me".

As my fingers traced the wooden craving, each grove telling a story of its own. Following the patterns of different flowers aligned with the butterflies flying above. What can this box hold? I didn't know what to expect. What can it be. The urge to unlock it's mysterious consumed me. As I started to approach the lock on the center. My mother halted my impulsive desires, asked me to go up to my room before I looked into it.

"You know what is there in this?" I asked

"Nani asked no one to open it before you, so ... strict orders from the headquarters" her words filled with respect for Grandma's wishes.

As I reached my room, which stood adjacent to Nani's own sacred space. I placed the box gently on the bed. However, before I could unlock the secrets within, I got an unexpected invitation to the temple. I wouldn't decline that.

I took a glimpse at the reflection at the bright yellow kurta and its white thread work placed on the corner of my cuff and my collar.

As I entered the gates of the temple, I couldn't help but be mesmerized by the delicate craftsmanship of the gate and the two pillars on each side,

but more than that I could see me, entering the temple with Nani by my side.

The love she had for them was boundless. She was(is) a beautiful soul.

All I know is because of the learnings I got from her, the early morning story session. Explaining the backstory of every festival.

Radha Krishn. How can I not mention them.

Isn't it beautiful - The forbidden love or maybe the way they express it.

I think I understand love because of them a little better.

This time I didn't have anything to pray for, this time I didn't plead for the wellbeing of anyone. (Nani maybe?) This time I decided to get astonished by the beautiful dance of life. The ups and downs. The pain and gain. The past and the present. The universe. And them

As I look deep into their eyes wondering if anyone could love anyone like they did. Will anyone love me like that, the undemanding love.

Isn't it beautiful,

I can't help but feel overwhelmed by the delicate and complexity of it all. It all seems vast and mysterious, yet I feel connected to all of it.

Sometimes it's hard to make sense of it all. But standing here, in front of Krishn, I don't feel alone in this journey. His peaceful presence reminds me to embrace every step through out.

As tears crease the corner of my smile, I wish to surrender to the universe -

I was zoned out for quite a bit when I realized it's time to leave.

Climbing down the stairs without turning my back to them. Facing them, as I placed my feet slowly, with each passing step I could see them disappearing.

When I came back, I was ready to open that box and be astonished for sure.

As I placed that box right in front of me. I unleashed the beauty within and there it was.

The red satin cloth was clanged to the inside of the box, as I could see the perfectly arranged envelopes, all crafted with Nani's letter set.

On the top was one letter with the date written on top of it and on the bottom right was written - read it when I am not there anymore.

NO WAY!

I couldn't adopt the idea of her not being around but now, the realisations of her absence struck me, the weight of her absence casting a shadow over the treasure she had left behind.

The paper felt fragile in my hands. As I gently opened the seal that guarded the secret within, anticipation fluttered in my chest like a cage of birds longing for release.

As my eyes trace the elegant script, a wave of emotions crashed over me, breaking down all the barriers. Each word was a brushstroke - a vivid picture of loss and love. Tears welled in my eyes, blurring the ink on the page but the ache in my soul sharpened.

Reading those words, I felt a flood of emotions wash over me.

In that moment, I realized the power of language to move us, to connect us, to remind us of the ones that came before us.

At that moment I knew that I would carry those words with me always, a reminder of beauty and pain.

In the quiet of the night, do you feel my silent cries,

Lost and hurting, beneath these darkened skies?
I'm tangled in pain, drowning in my fears,
Do you see the cracks in my heart, the tears in my soul,
Where can I find comfort in this empty space,
Can you imagine the weight of this never-ending ache,
How do I carry on without her by my side,
Her absence a wound, too deep to hide.
I wonder if she's watching from above,
In the quiet whispers, in the ones we love.

The letter

Dearest Sia

As I write these words, I am filled with a mix of emotions, knowing that at this exact time, when you are reading this, I won't be there with you. I wish I had all the answers about what comes after this life, but the truth is, none of us truly know.

However, if there's any chance of me watching over you from wherever I may be, I want you to know this - I looking down at you right now. I am smiling down at you, bursting with pride for the beautiful and incredible person you have grown into. Which I take all the credit for.

I wish I could have had this conversation with you in person but since it's not possible, I am leaving you this box filled with every lesson I wish u could've taught you about this journey called life. It's like a piece of me that you can hold onto whenever you need it.

You have been the reason for my smile since the very first day, Sia. Your phone calls or the dancing videos of yours (which your mother secretly kept sharing with me) kept me going on the toughest of times. I adore the love we share for all kind of things.

I know right now may seem hard but stay strong. I will always be with you in sprit. And if I have a say in it, I will be watching over every step of the way.

So, take this box, my dear. Open it when you need guidance, when you need a reminder of just how loved you are. Inside are all the lessons I have learnt though my journey, packaged up just for you.

Remember, life is a wild ride. There will be ups and downs, twists and turns, but though it all, never forget who you are. You are strong, you are capable and you are loved beyond measure and to be honest I love you calling me “sexy Nani”.

So, live your life to the fullest, my darling. Chase your dreams with all your heart, knowing that I am right beside you, guiding you and cheering you on.

With all my love,

Nani
Radhe Radhe

SIA

Two

As our hands accidentally touched, I stole a glance at him. Softly, he whispered those precious words, "I love you, Rose," and it felt like my stomach was suddenly doing somersaults. It was as if my heart had decided to put on a circus act right there in my chest.

But just as I was lost in the beautiful writing of this book I just started; my phone rudely interrupted with its "pling!" sound. I couldn't help but roll my eyes. Who could possibly be bothering me now? Tomorrow marks the big first day of high school, and my phone's buzzing with messages from people who barely know me, all offering condolences about my grandma's passing. It's nice, I guess, but it feels kind of hollow.

Reluctantly, I finally glanced at the screen, and for a split second, I forgot how to breathe. Goosebumps instantly appeared on my skin. It was a text from Raghav, the twin brother of my best friend Alaina. Calling him just a crush seems too simple; it's more like a tangled web of emotions. He's older than me, with these eyes that shine like warm cocoa. Whenever he looks at me, it's like I'm melting on the spot.

I often find myself wondering what it would be like to get lost in those eyes, to have those conversations that go so deep you lose track of time. But then reality hits – I'm stuck daydreaming while he's out there being the big shot basketball captain. And yet, amidst all his responsibilities, he remembered about our final game tomorrow.

"Good luck for your final match as a shooting stars' captain! " His text reads, and suddenly, my game face is back on. I completely forgot about the game. He's the captain of the high school team, and I'm leading the middle school girls' team. "Shooting Star," a name I tried to change but failed. Luckily, the high school teams called the Hawks – maybe that's a sign of what's to come.

As I prepare for high school, Raghav's message feels like a boost of confidence. It's like he's saying, "You've got this," and for that fleeting moment, I believe him. And maybe, just maybe, that's enough to carry me through.

"Make us proud star-y "

STARY!?

" I will try "

Try. I try.

" With you leading them, there's no chance of losing"

Ahhh the urge to tell him my feelings!

But I can’t. I have known him for 5 yrs. and he had been the only guy I ever felt that electric feeling in my blood. I first felt it in 7th grade (almost 3 yrs ago) when I was at sleep over at Alaina's and she slept early. I remember vividly, I couldn't sleep, so I tip-toed into the kitchen for some midnight cravings and there he was.

3 yrs ago ....

“Hey? what you doing, need anything " young Raghav said. with his dark curly hair covering most of his forehead and some of his eyes.

" I am sorry! Didn't mean to wake you up "

He did seem like I woke him up, with sleep sneaking into eyes.

"Oh no! Don't worry about it " ahh he's so cute.

" Want to eat something " he offered

"Actually, I was a bit hungry"

"Oh ok, what would you like. People say my noodles have magic "

Did someone ever mention to him about his dreamy voice!?

" That would be perfect" A very poor attempt to giggle

" A bowl of magic coming up"

While he cooked, we chatted and that's when I got to know about his love for basketball (that is also the reason I started playing it). When finally, he took out 2 bowls and served the delicious looking noodles. He said "wait a minute! "

He poured us some lemonade and I could see the excitement pouring out of his eyes as I had the first bite and he was right, it was amazing.

I looked up, sparkles in my eyes and I think that was enough for him to know that I loved it because he said

“ I told you I have magic "

Yes, he did

After that we couldn't realize when we spent the next 4 hrs talking and still after that we couldn't stop and that exact moment was when I got tangled in this web.

As number 3 passed the ball to me, the court went silent, we had 50 seconds left. 50 seconds to finals. 50 seconds as captain. 50 seconds to score 2 points.

I had a direct 3 pointer shot and I aimed and

Shot!

As the ball went straight, I could see the opponent player trying to stop it but she couldn't reach it.

As my feet landed, the ball went in and SCORE!

For the next 10 seconds it was still dead quiet and then

A hand came on my shoulder, and then everybody started cheering and yelling. Our coach presented us with the award and we all shook hands with the player from another team. The whole team hugged and that's when our coach screamed

" Rising to shine!"

Oh no! I hated this but it was officially the last time I ever have to say this

That's when everyone screamed together, not just the player but everyone from our school

"Like shooting stars in the sky"

As it ended, we all burst into laughter.

That's when I felt a pair of arms on my shoulders, as I turned back. It was him.

"Raghav! " I screeched

" Star-y! You kept your promise. I knew you could do it" he said

"Thanks " I chuckled nervously

" My house. Tonight. Have to celebrate this "

"That's a plan”.

"Sure is" he said while winking.

As he walked away, someone almost jumped on me. It was Alaina.

" I am so proud of you, champion. By the way did I see my brother. "

"Yes! He just wanted to congratulate me and invited me to your house tonight"

"Oh, did you have any plans to invite me as well"

" You can come if you want!" I spoke

" Tonight! It's set! We have so much to celebrate "

"Oh yes! What happened to your art exhibition " I asked

She started fidgeting with her fingers like she does when she is upset or nervous and then screamed in my ear " it was a hit!"

With the last scream of the day, we returned.

As I stuffed my bag with all kind of things - books, pens, face mask, camera and what not. Every time I go to their place for sleepover, I try to carry my whole room. It is very unpredictable what we will end up doing, so I want to be prepared. Now the last thing. Get ready! As I put on my red dress, clanged to my curves with scalping on the corners with my Black shiny sneakers. On my way out I totally forgot and ran back to my room and tucked the hair clutch to the sling of my bag.

The clutch belongs to Nani (grandma). I go nowhere without it. I feel safe with it.

RAGHAV

Three

I had an automatic smile on my face

Looking at her. Jumping around with no care in the world

I just looked but I couldn't get enough of it until I memorized every curve in her body and every inch of her smile.

She was formally just my sister's best friend but I think I can call her my friend now

We share a love for basketball. Seeing her on the court today. It was mesmerizing.

She had a sense of belonging when it comes to her loved ones. She rules on the court and I think that's the reason the coach made her captain in just 3 months of training.

Sia - I have seen her grow up. I have seen her laughing as she rolls on the floor and I have also seen her ugly cry.

As her luscious black curly hair falls down to her hips, she dances like every bone of her body feels the beat.

She doesn't dress up mostly when she comes over, but today I could see she had put thought

Into it.

I am happy she is enjoying herself, especially after these few weeks. She was dead scared about her grandma. I remember the late-night calls Alaina had every night, when her grandma wasn't well.

It was the 20th when she called,

Her voice breaking, "she passed away, I am on the way"

She was is hurry so before we could get a chance to comfort her, she hung up.

A night before she was sobbing "I am scared every time I see mom's number displayed on my phone"

She expressed "nobody knows when it's going to 'the call', I am not ready for it" she continued,

"The last time I spoke to her, we were discussing to plan a trip of hers to our place" she continued crying and none of us knew what to do.

It won't be long until she will be leading the hawks. She got the skills.

At this point, everyone had started making their way out, for what I know Sia is staying over.

"Clean up fast, mom and dad would kill us if they see this mess"

"What time are they arriving tomorrow?" Aliana asked,

"Noon" I replied as everyone left, we all started to clean up. I could hear both of them laughing and screaming like hyenas.

"We have time to clean up, ok snotty pants!" Aliana said trying to act all smart, Sia's giggling echoing in the background.

"you guys together? I might just kick back and get popcorn. Why don't you jazz up your cleaning skills" I say while rolling my eyes.

"Mr. captain clean freak!" she whispered loud enough for it to reach me.

When everything felt back at its place, I decided to work on my novel. I have been working on it from a month, it's nothing big but a little here and there. No one really knows about; I have decided to complete the manuscript before I tell anyone.

. As I sat down, fidgeted with my keyboard a little, words suddenly converted into sentences, sentences into paragraphs and paragraphs into a story. It's beautiful what magic words hold.

I started writing few years ago, I also had that one diary which held all my secrets. I never realised when my diary converted in to an application on my phone. My notes –

It was a few months back when books and words started to give me comfort, my curiosity grew and I sat and spent hours learning about literature and art of writing and publishing a book.

As my hand sprinted over the keyboard, I spent the next few hours, thinking, imagining and smiling over the screen filled with my pain and beauty.

As I stepped into the kitchen to grab a glass of lemonade, guess who I saw munching over a bag of chips. "What are you doing, Sia?!" not surprised.

"I am hungry" she declared, raising both her hands

As I make my way past her "move!"

I knew exactly what she needed, as I started to cook some noodles, Sia climbed up the counter and with her big googly eyes she took each step in.

With her, one can feel the most appreciated and adored. She misses no chance to express how proud she is or delighted she might be for our achievement is her own.

She had her blue pyjamas on, with white flower printed on them. As I follow her finger tips, they landed on the claw clip tucked onto her upper. “It was my grandma’s” she said, while I stared.

“Everyone decided to get something that belonged to her, I think everyone wanted a part of her with them, and I chose this”

“Why a claw clip?” I asked

” Because she has worn it enough for its two teeth to be missing. ‘cause her hands once embraced the butterfly on the top. ‘cause it belongs to her and I need her. I need her always to be clipped on to me”

She unclutched it and playfully clipped on to the front of my hair.

I caressed my face and popped my feet up from the ground, flexing my awesome look.

She laughed, and got her phone out to snap me.

And she laughed louder

“Shhhhhhhh! Shut up weasel!”

As I placed the food and lemonade on the coffee table, she sank into the couch. Anybody could see how tired she is, not just physically but emotionally.

I wish I could help her.

Be whatever she needs

"how's it" Recognizing that despite its potential shortcomings, she would still value it.

"Per-fect" she struggled while slurping on it.

She cracks me up.

Looking at her face, every inch of her mouth stuffed with noodles.

The spark in her eyes with every bite.

I follow and do the same.

"What were you doing this late?" she asked,

"Did I wake you up again" she continued.

"No, it wasn't you. I was- "

"Thank god!" she exclaimed.

We shared a laugh,

"How are you" I asked, soften my eyes.

"Great!" she replied, matching my intensity.

She knew what and why I was asking, I could see it in her eyes

She had a face which said more than her voice, though she is a never-ending radio box.

"Hey do you wish you had someone" she asked.

Someone? "What like"

"Maybe like a partner, half of my class got one" she explained

"How are you so sure that I don't one"

"Come on! We had a party tonight and not one person, in specific, not one girl seemed like your date."

Yeah, it's true, I don't have a girlfriend. But I'm not rushing into anything. Maybe I'm a bit scared too. Love can be really scary sometimes. It's like this big unknown, you know? And it's not just scary; it can make you feel like you're going crazy. One moment you're fine, and the next, you're all over the place, thinking about this person all the time, wondering if they feel the same way. It's a rollercoaster of emotions. But I think that's what makes it so exciting too. It's like diving into the deep end of a pool without knowing how to swim. You're scared, but there's this thrill that comes with it. So, yeah, I don't have a girlfriend, and maybe I'm scared, but I'm also kind of excited to see where this all goes. Because who knows? Maybe love isn't as scary as we think.

"Maybe"

"I wish I had one" she exclaimed.

SIA

Four

As I made my way towards English, Alaina joined me.

Her shirt filled with spots of paint gave me an idea of where she is coming from, "An hour of creativity?" I give off my 'where were you, I hated it without you' look.

As I stepped into English class, a subtle hum of conversation enveloped me, piquing my curiosity. There was an energy in the air, and I couldn't help but wonder what it was about. Thoughts raced through my mind; however, I couldn't ignore the possibility that word had spread about my winning shot in yesterday's match. The idea brought a rush of excitement and nerves. With each passing moment, the rumours seemed to grow, painting me as the hero of the game. A warm smile spread across my face as I relived the moment in my mind. Despite the close quarters of the classroom, I found myself embracing the attention, a sense of pride and satisfaction washing over me.

That's when our teacher entered and we all made our way to out places. Me and Alaina slid and sat together, hoping our teacher doesn't notice (yesterday's howling like hyenas didn't help with it). As she starts "Sia?" she grabs my attention.

"Great work on the court" she announced, finishing with a smile filled with pride.

As some mocked me, Alaina mocks them back "I can smell jealously" she mouthed wile smirking.

Ten minutes into the class, a loud knock jolted us, drawing our attention to the gate. There he stood, resembling someone who had just emerged from court. As he entered, his gaze fixed on me, he handed the teacher a note,

"Sia, you are excused. Your excellence from the last match is still lurking within our school's court." passing a gentle smile.

" Great! thank you ma'am" he said.

I stood up, grabbing my bag. I went to Raghav.

While I minded my steps until I left my classroom.

I couldn't wonder what it was and I think it was too obvious.

"it's nothing, don't worry, the coach wants to meet you''

"Me?"

As we went into the court,

It was much better than the middle school court, I had come here multiple times, for camps, practise match and for Raghav's matches.

It smelled so clean.

The coach and a few girls stood around them,

As the caught my sight,

"Raghav! And you must be Sia" coach exclaimed.

"Yes sir" I said feeling a little flourish in gut.

"Of course, we know all about you-" he said.

I bowed a little while placing my right hand onto my left shoulder.

"Sid has mentioned you several times" he continued

I looked at him give him a 'thank you and 'I am surprised'' look. It rather seemed like he didn't care and continued looking at coach's direction.

"As we transition into a new semester, with the departure of our senior comrades. Now, with just two juniors left in the ranks, it's time to roll up our sleeves and get down to business. After all, the shoes we're filling are big ones." he said while looking at me and one other girl, who seemed a year older.

I was still confused. Did I just make the high school? I am hawk now!

"Normally we get enough time to form a team before the inter school basketball championship but apparently this time we won't have enough time. This year its in 2 months, for both girls and boys and my boys' team are ready....?" He said with a hint of confusion and that's when Raghav said

"Yes. YES!"

"Good! Now we need to prep the girls' team and I need you and you in it" again pointing at both of us "and Sid you need to help them along the way"

"Sure thing, coach"

That's when coach left us alone in there. I looked at Sid and

"Ok I am on the squad?"

"Wait! We have the most important championship in 2 months with 2 members?"

"I have to help with building a team?"

"And ....am I missing something?" I finished

"Nahh! Though it was entertaining, seeing you freak!"

I just continued to stare at him till I could laser a hole into his head.

I didn't know what I could do.

SIA

Five

Sitting alone in my room, clutching the letter tightly, I'm suddenly joined by my mother, a pillar of strength since our earliest days. Her presence alone is a comfort. She's not just a mother; she's my eternal companion.

Whenever life throws challenges at us, her arms were our sanctuary. But despite her unwavering support, I can't shake the nagging doubt that no matter how hard I try, I'll always fall short. It's a feeling that gnaws at me, a relentless whisper that I'll never measure up.

Yet, in her eyes, I see only love and pride. She doesn't judge me by some unattainable standard. To her, I am already enough. It's a truth I struggle to accept, lost amidst my own insecurities.

In this quiet moment, as she stands beside me, her mere presence is a reminder of her boundless love. She's not looking for perfection; she secks only my happiness. And perhaps, in her strong belief in me, I can find the strength to believe in myself too.

We are really similar -her and me. we feel a lot (which in her view is a weakness) but the only difference is, she hides it under her thick Armor, whereas I am learning to embrace it every day.

SIA

Six

As we all entered the great hall to assemble. I spotted Raghav and coach near the podium, from my previous incidents, it's always something unexpected once they both come along.

Raghav approached once the other announcements ever over.

"Good morning athletes,

I am here to announce that try outs for the girls' basketball team will be held tomorrow after school in the gymnasium. Led by Sia, Zara," so that's what her name was

"And myself, this is an opportunity for you to showcase your skills, teamwork, and commitment to the sport. Whether you're a seasoned player or new to basketball, we encourage everyone to participate

Please arrive prepared with appropriate athletic attire. We look forward to seeing your skills and dedication on the court. And remember" he hesitated saying whatever he was going to, looking at coach for reassurance, "teamwork is dream work"

Team work is dream work ?? now I get it why he didn't want to say it.

As we leaped into the corridors, my sight landed on the board, fumed with different flyers and notices, updates of what new is going on. The board's each corner seemed to be seeking some information. In the centre, one shiny brand-new notice glared straight at me, it was drawing me enough to stop and read it,

****

NOTICE!!

The dance committee wants to host a formal dinner for all the highschoolers, for our thought into turn into reality, we will need your help. Kindly spare a moment and join us in the dance club after school

1pm - 2pm

We will be waiting for you!

Until then, FEEL THE BEAT

Regards

Dance club!

****

Oh my god! I need this. I mentally planned to go there anyhow.

That's when Raghav caught up, these might the best days of my life, suddenly Raghav is far more interested in talking to me than ever, maybe it's just cause of basketball. Of course, its cause of basketball. I mentally slapped myself into reality. He stood beside me, rubbing the back of his head, and I could tell he was anticipating a comment on the speech he had just given—a compliment, to be clear.

"So," he said with an almost puppy-like expression,

"Teamwork is dre-"

"What do you expect me to do? Coach asked me to," he interrupted, perhaps a bit too abruptly.

"Is that so?" my shoulders slumped a bit, and my tone deflated. "Makes much more sense."

I noticed the disappointment in his voice and softened my own. "Hey, it's not about what I expect, it's about what you believe in. And your commitment to the team really shines through in your words."

A hint of a smile returned to his face. "Thanks, man. Means a lot."

As he stood beside me, his laughter echoed through the room, wrapping us in its comforting embrace. My stomach did somersaults, a flurry of butterflies fluttering wildly within me, as his infectious joy washed over me. His eyes, a deep and captivating shade of brown, held a magnetic pull that drew me closer, revealing layers of complexity beneath their sparkling surface.

His tousled chestnut hair framed his face in a casually tousled manner, adding to his effortless charm.

Despite my attempts to keep my composure, I found myself irresistibly drawn to him. His laughter, so genuine and carefree, ignited a warmth within me that I couldn't ignore. And when our eyes met, it was as though time stood still, allowing us to share a moment of unspoken understanding.

In that fleeting moment, the laughter and exchanged glances, I couldn't deny the growing attraction I felt for him. It wasn't just his laughter or his gaze, but the way he seemed to light up the room with his presence.

“By the way” him pulling me back to reality

“You have to come after to school to gym to prep for tomorrow”

“Raghav! Did you see the flyer about the dance the dance committee is hosting” of Couse I wanted to go with him, there’s nobody else I think about.

“Yes?”

“I was thinking about going there today”

“Why??”

“I like their idea; I want to be a part of that”

Raghav 's eyebrows shot up in surprise as I mentioned the dance committee. "Wait, you're actually thinking of joining that?"

I nodded enthusiastically, my excitement bubbling over. "Absolutely! I mean, why not? It could be a fun way to break up the monotony of basketball practice, don't you think?"

Sid's expression darkened, a frown creasing his brow. "Fun? We have try-outs tomorrow, and you're talking about joining a dance committee?"

I bristled at his tone, feeling defensive. "Come on, Raghav. It's not like I'll be there while you're out there shooting hoops. I'll still be giving it my all at practice."

He crossed his arms, unconvinced. "It's not just about practice, you know. We need to be focused and in sync, we have these important matches coming up, adding more distractions won't help. It's about the time, it's about where your priorities are. "

I sighed, feeling a twinge of frustration. "I get it, Raghav, but I really want to go for this."

Raghav ran a hand through his hair, his expression softening slightly. "I guess I just don't want to see you spread yourself too thin. You're already juggling school, basketball, and everything else. Adding dance into the mix seems like a recipe for disaster."

I chuckled, rolling my eyes. "Disaster? Please, I'm not that bad. Besides, it's just one hour after school. I'm sure I can handle it."

Raghav sighed, his shoulders slumping in defeat. "Fine. Do what you want. Just don't come crying to me when you're too tired to keep up with practice."

As we walked away, I couldn't shake the feeling of disappointment that lingered in the air

****

SIA

Seven

As I suited up in my jersey, nerves jittering like popcorn in a microwave, I caught my reflection and couldn't help but second-guess my recent snack choices. "Man, I should've had fewer midnight snacks," I mused.

Entering the gym, I spotted Raghav, casually tossing hoops. "Shooting some hoops, Raghav?" I hollered, strutting over and swiping the ball before he could protest. As I dashed towards the hoop, I could almost hear the crowd cheering in the background. With a flick of the wrist, the ball sailed through the net, and I erupted into a victory dance, waving my hands like I was trying to summon a genie.

Soon, the gym started to buzz. I beamed at Raghav, super excited–until I overheard some hushed whispers. Turns out, half the town showed up for Raghav's spectacle. Apparently, I wasn't the only one mesmerized by his charm.

As we stood, our eyes stuck to the gate, it dawned on me: Raghav wasn't just a basketball player; he was a magnet for admirers, drawing them in like moths to a particularly handsome flame.

We started with simple exercises, followed by drills, the gym alive with energy

Me and Raghav started to show others different ways to shot, dribble and pass.

Raghav, with his effortless grace and skill, effortlessly commanded attention. His every move on the court seemed to carry an aura of confidence, drawing the gaze of admirers. As he effortlessly sank shot after shot, his presence seemed to electrify the atmosphere.

Meanwhile, I nervously bounced the basketball in my hands, trying to steady my racing heart. The pressure was palpable as I watched Raghav effortlessly showcase his talent. Doubt crept into my mind as I wondered if I could ever measure up to his skill and charisma.

Each player showcased their skills, determination shining through with every move. The sound of dribbling balls and cheering filled the air.

I could see a team build already.

Everybody had their own energy

We continued with some team building exercises,

Which would help us figure the chemistry

As the try outs progressed, it became increasingly clear that we were not just a group of individuals vying for a spot on the team; we were becoming a team in our own right. There was an unspoken understanding among us, a shared determination to succeed not just for ourselves but for each other.

The energy on the court was infectious, spreading from player to player like wildfire. It was in the high-fives exchanged after a successful play, the words of encouragement shouted across the court, and the smiles shared during breaks.

By the end of the try outs, it felt like we had already built something special—a foundation of trust. And as we walked off the court, exhausted but exhilarated, we knew that no matter what the future held, we had already achieved something remarkable: we had become a team.

" Great work everybody" Raghav said loudly, I think it swept in.

Raghav stepped closer to me and whispered, "you should say something to everyone"

I wished Zara wouldn't have bailed on us.

I spoke up, "Wow, everyone, seriously, amazing stuff out there today. You all brought your A-game, and honestly, it's going to be super tough to pick the final squad. But hey, that's a good problem to have, right? I just want to say a huge thanks to each and every one of you for showing up and giving it your all.

Tomorrow's the final try out, and I know it's going to be even more intense, but hey, that's where champions are made, right? So, let's rest up, hydrate, maybe get some extra shots in if you can, and let's come back tomorrow ready to leave it all on the court. Great job today, everyone!" I looked in Raghav's direction for confirmation.

When I saw a girl in hot pink matching sports-wear enter, looking in rush. I couldn't see her vividly.

I really should start wearing my glasses more often.

"today's try outs are out" I spoke in her direction

It was Aanya,

I blanked out, it happens every time I see her. She 'was' my best friend. Emphasis on was.

SIA

Eight

Maybe I can never be poetry. Maybe I always have to be scribble, the ones before the perfect lines are formed. The ones that are somewhere there but not exactly rhythmic.

I believe I wasn't taught about the depth of a simple word " friendship". Today as I look deep in my cell as its light is injecting straight into my eyes. Trying to understand where it all went wrong.

Why does no one talk about the way few friends become a part of you and your soul. Just like Voldemort's horcrux. I hoped someone would have taught me that before I started stepping into making my own world. I was taught the importance of family, money, values, studies, and power but never in my life did someone came up to me saying " You might get someone in your life who understands you like a sister, takes care of you like a mother, protect you like a brother, scolds you like a father and spoils you like your grandparents, but still won't be a part of your family but won't be anything less than that. You might get 10 or maybe just one of them, but you should always cherish them, because sometimes they will be all you will ever need"

So now, I will try again. It's my attempt million before I allow myself to let go, let go of the memories, the phone calls, the screenshots of every paragraph he ever wrote for me, the last 2 years and of another part of my SOUL. Leaving you with letters I wrote and with the ones you wrote me. Leaving after you became a habit while I became yours.

Flashback!

It wasn't just Alaina from the very beginning. I had another group of friends once, buy slowly they drifted away, leaving me feeling like I had been abandoned. It was definitely a tough pill to swallow. Looking at their group photos now, without me was a punch in the gut. Everyone else seemed to see it coming but I was completely blindsided

The breaking point came on Aanya's birthday, which fell on 2nd July. I remember stepping outside to take a call, thinking nothing of it. Completely unaware of what waited for me. But when I returned after just ten minutes, the atmosphere had shifted dramatically. Silence filled the room, and all eyes were on me.

"Hey, why don't you go check outside?" someone suggested.

Confused, I asked, "Check for what?"

"Just go!" another insisted urgently.

Feeling a knot forming in my stomach, I found a spot-on a nearby couch. They laughed and exchanged mocking remarks about me, each word like a dagger to my heart. As the minutes passed, the laughter seemed to intensify, their voices growing louder and more piercing.

After thirty minutes, then forty-five, and still, it didn't stop. I was on the verge of tears, feeling betrayed and alone. I reached out to Alaina, my closest confidante, begging her to come.

Fifty minutes later, I couldn't bear to stay any longer. Summoning what little courage I had left, I pushed open the door and stepped in, my voice barely above a whisper.

"I'm leaving," my words drowned out by their laughter.

I couldn't wait for a reply.

With trembling steps, I made my way to Alaina's waiting car, grateful for her comforting presence. As we drove away, it felt as though years of friendship had crumbled before my eyes, replaced by hurt and anger.

That day marked the end of an era, a bitter realization that sometimes, even the closest bonds can fracture.

That day and today
Everyone moved on but I think I stuck around.
It's more like -
"I am always there for you ",
We said it a million times
but you left, there's no deny.
Wherever I tried I felt my
Foot stuck to the ground
With the glue of time.
Then I saw those eyes,
I couldn't help myself
But feel alive.
However, why does it
Pierce my heart, straight as a line.
It's been days, weeks and months now,
But my heart is still holding a welcome sign.
I am always there for you
and that was never a lie.

RAGHAV

Nine

I could see the light vanish from her eyes, as I turned my head to the left, I understood why.

Aanya was standing Infront of us, with a blink Sia hid her feelings.

"Sorry I am late" Aanya spoke.

"We just wrapped up" I interfered.

"Maybe we can give a chance. Let her show what she got" said Sia, always the optimist.

I could see Aanya roll her eyes, which actually made my blood boil. Aanya left her in a bad position and I wasn't about forgive and forget.

Breakup of friendship can tear people and mess them up and I hate that Sia had to face it, multiple times.

Sia always believed in people, no matter how long she knew them.

"Sure, why not? Just because you said so," I nodded, giving in reluctantly.

I actually never knew Aanya ever played ball.

We performed few drills and involved everyone, though I hate saying it but. she was. great.

We could totally use someone like her in the squad. She knew her stuff

I could she Sia getting scared but I also could see the proud feeling flickering in her eyes. She was so happy being around or we can say playing with her.

“Okay” I got all the attention. I was loving the attention; I could clearly see the juniors and others drooling. It was fun and all but on the court all that was the least of my worries.

I clapped my hand twice before continuing, “I think everyone is exhausted.”

“Let’s end it for today, you will be notified about the list of final call back till tomorrow morning.

Kindly look into it”

"We will see you all tomorrow, please be on time" Sia said before walking up to Alaina.

I headed to change, "Sia!" I called out.

"I have to wait after changing to discuss the list. Right?" she said. Like she knew everything.

I hesitated "yes". This girl blows me away.

****

We sat and started debating. Everyone bought something great to the table, even the ones who knew nada about the play. After several pointers we were able to draft a list

While Sia took a glimpse at the list, I spoke up.

"You know, we can substitute Aanya"

"No and that's not why I am- "

"Tensed! I think the word you are looking for is tensed" Alaina butted in.

"She knew I am a part of it but still she showed up" she finished.

"You know, not everyone makes decisions based on what others think, unlike you." I confessed

I hated how Aanya affected her so much.

****

SIA

Ten

You know, I've been thinking, 'weird' doesn't really feel like an insult to me. It's like this word holds something special, you know? Like, 'weird' could mean so much more than just being strange.

I mean, I've been called 'weird' plenty of times. I guess I am kind of weird—I'm a mix of too much and not enough. Sometimes I'm super excited about stuff, other times I feel like I'm way too serious for my age. And sure, maybe I don't fit the typical mold. Maybe I've got a big nose, or my eyebrows are a little funky, or I might have too chubby cheeks. But hey, that's just me.

I might be too giggly, or my hugs might be a bit too tight. Maybe I'm not everyone's cup of tea. But you know what? That's okay. Because being 'weird' is just part of who I am. It's what makes me, well, me. And honestly, I wouldn't have it any other way.

But being 'weird' isn't always easy. It's like you're constantly trying to fit in, to be like everyone else, but at the same time, you're trying to figure out who you really are. And sometimes, that can be a real struggle.

There are days when I feel like I'm too much, like I don't belong anywhere. I worry that people will judge me or laugh at me because I'm not like them. It's hard not to compare myself to others, to wish I could be more like the popular kids or the ones who seem to have it all figured out.

But then I remember that being 'weird' isn't a bad thing. It's what makes me unique, what sets me apart from the crowd. And yeah, it might be tough sometimes, but it's also kind of liberating. I don't have to pretend to be someone I'm not, or hide parts of myself just to fit in.

It's okay life scares you right now and you don't have all the answers. It's okay if everything feels overwhelming and you're not sure what to do next. It's okay if every step feels like you're walking through a storm of anxiety, and fear.

You don't have to pretend that everything is okay when it's not. It's okay to feel scared, anxious, or worried. All those feelings are valid, and they have value. Sometimes, our greatest strength lies not in pretending everything is fine, but in acknowledging our pain and struggles.

After the chaos settles and the storm clouds clear, you will rise, stronger and wiser than before.

So, feel what you need to feel. Do what heals you. Accept yourself, exactly as you are, with all your fears, flaws, and imperfections. You are enough, just as you are. And you will get through this, one step at a time.

So yeah, being 'weird' has its challenges, but it's also a source of strength. It's a reminder that I don't have to conform to society's expectations, that I can embrace my quirks and flaws and still be proud of who I am. And in the end, isn't that what really matters?

People are like rivers, always moving, always changing. They're never really fixed in one place. You might think you know them, but they're constantly shifting. And whatever you try to hold onto, it just gets swept away. It's like they're here one moment and gone the next.

RAGHAV

Eleven

We ever able to understand everyone's gameplay when we dismissed them.

I glanced across the gym, and once again, my eyes landed on her. She was a regular sight here, always showing up early and leaving late ever since the try-outs were announced. Today, I decided to make my move, determined to crack that tough exterior of hers.

With my most charming smile stuck on my face, I went over, ready to introduce myself. But her response? A poisonous poker face. Not even a flicker of interest. Regardless of, I pressed on, asking for her name, while I shared mine

"Shara," she muttered, barely audible. It seemed like she was ready to bolt, pulling her hood up like a shield. But I wasn't about to let her off the hook that easily.

"Into basketball?" I shot her a questioning look, hoping for something more than a nod.

Surprisingly, she nodded, just a hint of interest there, bullseye! So, I grabbed the ball nearby and signed for her to join me on the court. As she stepped forward, I handed her the ball, fully expecting to give her some pointers. But before I could say a word, she surprised me with a swift elbow jab, not enough to knock me out but definitely enough to make a point: she didn't need my help.

Well, okay then. I backed off, watching as she effortlessly handled the ball like a pro.

"You play?" I couldn't help but ask, genuinely impressed.

"I did," came her cool reply, eyes fixed on the ball like it held all the answers.

"I could see that," I said, a grin tugging at my lips. I was tempted to invite her to join our practice, but before I could, she was off, grabbing her bag and making a swift exit like she had some urgent mission to attend to.

Later, when I mentioned her to Sia, it turned out she'd noticed Shara too. It seemed like everyone was intrigued by this mystery girl, leaving me to wonder what her deal was and if I'd ever figure it out.

****

The following day, I sauntered into the gym with my team, and there she was, posted up with her notebook, quietly taking in the scene. Every now and then, she'd scribble something down, her gaze piercing, like she was dissecting our very souls. I swallowed my curiosity and honed in on the game, but her presence lingered in the back of my mind, a mystery begging to be unravelled.

As we ended our practice after a few quarters, Shara pulled her hood to cover her round face again and started to make her way to the exit,

"Not gonna stay for another team?" referring to the girl's team I said while slurping on water.

I almost thought that she won't she reply, as I turned around losing hope for a reply, I heard

"Not today."

I guess not today.

As she reached the gate,

Sia almost tackled into her.

"Excuse me-" whispered Shara. "sorry" they both said at the same time, followed by a small giggle.

"Shara. Right?"

"Yes" her voice still not raising above a whisper.

"I heard about you kicking Raghav's ass on court yesterday" Ouch! It was clearly because of my pointers.

She laughed louder than before.

Bullseye! Whatever breaks down her tough layer of whatever pride it is.

"Come on, show me those moves of yours on the court" she smoothing pitching it in.

"I don't play anymore"

She played yesterday and didn't have any problem while elbowing me down-

"Even yesterday it was just one short and it has been months since I stepped onto the court"

Was it just me but I could see her chin wombling.

"Umm...being honest, we were wondering-" Sia tried saying

"See ya around" I interrupted.

I walked towards the court as I forced Sia to turn around by the shoulder.

"What was that!" Sia barked.

"I don't. -

It doesn't seem as simple as just asking her" I said, almost not knowing what I was saying.

"Bruh! What is that supposed to mean"

****

I stood there in silence as coach joined us for today's practise

"Great job! the team seems to be in great shape"

I could see a spark in Sia's eyes as she smiled brightly.

"Now let's see what the team looks on the court.

6 may pick blue over t-es and others may take red."

Once the coach understood they wouldn't be able to choose, after seeing them almost killing each other,

Coach assigned it himself,

"These teams will be the same for the time being.

Blue team will be led by" passing an eye around.

"let's play one game and then choose the captains" coach finished and clapped his hand twice to get their attention (I learnt this from him).

He discussed rules, I could see him taking mental notes about everyone, reading everyone's body movement.

As the match started on his whistle,

I noticed Sia and Anaya being on the same team,

It's true Sia was one of the best players on the court right now (I might be a little bias),

I followed the ball around court when it was in Sia's hand, I popped my head out a little trying to transport all my energy into her, whatever that is.

As she leaped towards the hoop, I could clearly see Aanya cringe, though they were on the same team.

As the game went on, Sia really stood out with her amazing performance. Aanya even managed to score a few points herself. Sia, being her usual self, cheered the loudest and her eyes showed real kindness.

"Good game" coach shouted.

As he dismissed everybody,

"Raghav! Meet me at 5" he said as he left.

****

SIA

Twelve

As we left the court, I tried flashing a smile at Aanya. FAIL!

In the garden outside, I could see her sitting Shara.

I have to try again. I try to look as confident I can and walk towards her and try to shoot a conversation.

As I sat there,

"Hey there"

"hi" she responded.

"I know practise is over but, few hoops won't hurt" I said trying to sound cheerful.

As I waited for the perplexed expression on his face to dissipate, my fingers instinctively reached out and plucked the last remaining white flower from the sprawling bush behind us. Its delicate petals felt cool against my skin, a stark contrast to the warmth of the afternoon sun.

Examining the flower closely, I couldn't help but notice its fragile beauty.

“I would rather pass!”

“Oh, but...- “

“Hey, I use to play basketball but now it’s not my thing”

I could see her fidgeting with her fingers,
While stabbing her thumb's nail deep into her skin.
Why does she hurt herself like that? I wonder,
Is it because she feels lost within?
Does she think that pain will make her feel alive?
Or maybe it's a way to numb the pain inside.
But each time she cuts, does she realize,
It's just a temporary fix, a fleeting disguise?
I wish she could see the beauty in her scars,
Not as marks of weakness, but of battles fought.
And though she may feel broken
But maybe she's too lost to see,
That she's worth more than the scars she bears.

“Come on!” I pleaded

We're in dire need of a standout player, an under-the-radar gem. She's a fresh face, a newcomer to our school, and I see an opportunity. All day, I've been throwing her puppy-dog eyes, observing her every move. Perhaps through careful scrutiny, I can gauge her potential on the basketball court.

In the final period, I found myself facing her. As her eyes flashed with anger, she abruptly rose from her seat and approached me.

a smile gracing my lips.

“Stop!” she almost screamed.

It was the loudest she has ever been.

“.....”

“See I understand you-.” She stopped.

She continued “Wait, why are you so desperate about me playing”.

I'm feeling this strong conviction that she's meant to be part of our squad. It's like a gut instinct, pulling at me relentlessly. I'm certain she belongs here, destined to contribute to our success on the basketball court.

“I don’t know. But I know you are meant to be there. Why don’t you just give it a try.”

"Will it make you get off my back and stop acting like a desperate loser?" she said with a smirky smile.

I vigorously nodded.

"Tomorrow morning 6a.m. Don't be late!" She spun away without pausing for my response.

Bullseye!

This was going to be fun.

SIA

Thirteen

"Yeah!"

"Great shot, Shara!" I cheered as she effortlessly sunk the straight three-pointer, her skill evident even in our first practice together. With a wide smile, she dribbled the ball back to me, and I eagerly accepted the pass, feeling a surge of excitement.

Dribbling down the court, I couldn't shake off the nerves, but Shara's encouraging gaze spurred me on. As I approached the three-point line, determination overtook my apprehension. With a deep breath, I released the ball towards the hoop, hoping for the best.

The sound of the ball swishing through the net filled me with an exhilarating rush of accomplishment. "Yes!"

I exclaimed, my heart pounding with excitement. With every cheer and high-five exchanged.

As we caught our breath, the realization dawned on me- I got to have her in our team

Shara's beauty was as attracting as her skills on the court, she exuded an effortless grace that drew attention wherever she went. Her almond-shaped eyes sparkled with warmth, reflecting her passion for the game. Dark, flowing locks framed her face like silk, adding to her magnetic presence.

Her olive-toned skin glowed, adorned with delicate jewellery that danced with each movement,

But it wasn't just her physical beauty that made Shara stand out–it was the confidence and inner strength that radiated from within her. With every dribble and shot.

"It's almost time for practice. Everyone must be arriving in 10" I said

"Oh! Thanks, it was just amazing playing again."

"What if you stay for one match?" I said emphasizing on "please!".

"I don't think so, you all have important matches coming and you must need as much as time you could get for practice." She said, I almost felt as in she didn't want to be play

"But I am sure they would love seeing you fly through the court" Attempting to persuade her to agree.

"I am sorry I don't think I am ready!" she declared.

"Come o- "

"You asked for one match and here I am. I gotta go but thanks, it was fun" she ran to the exit.

I have to stop her and that means.

"How long will you run from the court! I know it's hard but I am sure this is what your dad wanted" ok. I regrated saying it the min it came out but I could think of nothing better.

SHARA

Fourteen

"DAD!"

"You have to come!" I exclaimed, desperation creeping into my voice.

"I have to rest, kid," Dad said, his voice strained from coughing.

"As my father and my coach, I can't play without you," I insisted, pointing directly at him.

"But-"

"You promised to be there for every game of mine," I reminded him, my words tinged with disappointment.

Dad's eyes softened as he looked at me,

"I know, kiddo," he said, his voice gentle

I hesitated,

"Okay, Dad," trying to mask my disappointment with a forced smile. "Just take care of yourself, alright?"

Dad nodded, a grateful smile tugging at the corners of his lips.

****

This was the first match dad ever missed before the huge list that followed.

I changed schools, hoping to start fresh, leaving behind the weight of expectations and preconceptions that had followed me. But as I stood in the assembly hall, surrounded by unfamiliar faces, a sense of longing struck within me when the announcement for basketball try-outs echoed through the room.

Despite my efforts to distance myself from my past, the urge to go to the basketball court remained irresistible. It was a place where I felt at home, where the rhythm of the game drowned out the noise of the world, and where my skills spoke louder than any rumours or judgments.

The thought of stepping onto the court again filled me with a mixture of excitement.

Proving myself all over again.

Basketball was more than just a sport to me; it was a part of who I was.

****

"DAD!?"

How does she know anything about it.

I looked back before I backed out and went back inside.

As Raghav entered the gym, his warm smile caught me off guard, causing a subtle blush to creep onto my cheeks. There was something about the way he looked at me.

As he began to divide us into groups, when it became apparent that our group was short of players, Raghav didn't hesitate to step in and join. Suddenly, he was standing right behind me, his existence sending my heart into a frenzy of beats.

I tried to focus on the drills and the game at hand.

As we moved through, I found myself drawn to Raghav's infectious enthusiasm. Whether he was offering advice on technique or cheering us on from the side.

In that moment, surrounded by the sounds of sneakers squeaking on the hardwood and the rhythmic thud of basketballs hitting the floor, I couldn't help but follow his every move.

Stepping back onto the basketball court after what felt like an eternity was both exhilarating and bittersweet. The echoes of my dad's coaching and encouragement seemed to linger in

With each dribble, each shot, it was as if the very act of playing the game I loved was a tribute to my dad, I could almost hear his voice cheering me.

With each pass and each basket, the weight of grief began to lift. Returning to the court felt like coming home.

SIA

Fifteen

What determines a good person-

Is it praying every day?

Or having the same friends for years?

It's a simple question, yet its answer seems blur to me like a wisp of smoke slipping through my fingers.

not yet fully aware of the complexities of the world, but old enough to recognize its shades of gray. This question sometimes seems to be revolving around my mind, maybe it's because I'm trying to figure out who I want to be, what values I want to uphold, and how I want to navigate this life.

I've always been told that goodness lies in actions, in kindness, in the way we treat others. And I believe that to be true to some extent. Holding the door open for someone, lending a helping hand, or simply offering a smile can all be gestures of goodness.

But then there's this nagging feeling that there's more to it than just actions. Goodness feels deeper. It's about the intentions behind those actions, isn't it? It's about seeing the world through someone else's eyes, even if their perspective differs from our own.

It's like this goodness, this light that shines brightly even in the darkest of times.

Perhaps goodness is about standing up for what we believe in, even if it means standing alone. It's about being honest, not just with others, but with ourselves.

But then again, maybe goodness is subjective. Maybe it means something different to each person, shaped by our experiences, our beliefs, and our upbringing. Maybe there's no one-size-fits-all answer to this question.

Maybe goodness is a journey, not a destination. Maybe it's about working on ourselves to be better each day, to learn from our mistakes.

So, what makes a person good? I'm not entirely sure yet. But maybe that's okay. Maybe the beauty lies in the search for the answer, in the conversations we have,

For every incomplete conversation which I am still finding an answer to .

RAGHAV

Sixteen

I knocked really hard.

"May I enter" I said as approached vice principal's cabin.

I took a seat,

"So, how's the work?"

"It's... going. At times I am stuck" I responded.

"It's you first so you will slowly catch on. You will understand your style"

"I just hope I don't mess up. I don't want you to regret it"

"I am teaching here for..." he paused to count "9 years now, and I never approached anyone before.

So, I am pretty sure of my decision."

I scooped into my bag and got a bunch of papers,

"These are somewhat 7 chapters!"

"I get back to you after I finish reading it"

As I leave, it hits me,

Alaina got her exhibition today.

I processed to the workshop,

"Hey!" I heard her chirping.

Sia caught up with me, "art studio?" she asked while raising her eyebrow.

"Yes, coming from practise?"

"Yup! I had hurry!"

"I can see that. You know you could have freshened up!" I was obviously teasing her, never in my life has she not smelled like literal vanilla.

"What! Shut up."

I knew I got to her. After seeing her conscious for 2 mins I said

"You smell fine, stop it or your vein will pop"

She just gave me an annoyed look and leaped forward.

As we went entered, Alaina stood in front of what seemed like a room slashed with ketchup and mustard.

Though it was beautiful; stalls of goodies or the paintings

Alaina led us up to her corner and as usual Sia was on the urge to tear up and I looked at them like a sore thumb. The last time Sia stomped on my feet, just so I give some reaction.

She took out a rectangle piece of what I could only guess as a canvas due to the surrounding.

It was gift wrapped with a classic brown vintage looking sheet and white ribbon which was lying on the ground once it came was handed to Sia.

As I slipped a glance over, I was startled by the awful scream or we can gasp proudly produced by the jumping and screaming rabbit standing by me.

Ok! I agree it was pretty impressive. The rectangle thing was indeed a canvas but the utterly arranged splash of paint was a portrait of Sia and Alaina.

On the corner it was written 'happy 16th'

WAIT! Is it her birthday today? It can't be, I haven't heard both these jackals laugh or scream like maniacs for quite a bit.

I opened my calendar and looked for it.

Ok its tomorrow! I have no idea now I forgot.

I grabbed Alaina by the sleeve and pulled her, "So what have we planned for her birthday"

"We!? There is no we mister. However, I have planned out everything" she said while smiling ear to ear.

"Come on, think about it.

She would feel so bad if she figures that I forgot her birthday, which I didn't not." I pulled the best puppy dog face I had.

"Ok ok, stop sulking. Listen carefully. I have planned night's stay with cake, pizza and of course her favourite rom-com."

"that's all. We have to go all out" I advised

"don't you know her at all, stop using your pea brain and let me handle." Who does she think she is.

As she joined Sia, I planned to do something on my own.

SIA

Seventeen

You promised, didn't you? You promised you'd never miss my birthday. But today, today you didn't call. Today, you didn’t sing "Happy Birthday" at the top of your lungs, trying to control your laughter, making me giggle uncontrollably.

Now, as the phone remains silent and there's no song to sing, I feel a load of sadness wash over me. I miss your warmth, your laughter, your stories that always seemed to make everything better.

I hold onto these letters of yours, reading and rereading them, but it's not the same, is it? It's not the same as having you here with me, laughing and singing and

I miss you more than words can express, Grandma. I miss your gentle smile, your comforting embrace, your unwavering love. And on this day, when I should be celebrating another year of life, I find myself wishing for the one thing on my candles I can't have–your presence.

****

As we dug into the cake, Alaina practically smashed a huge piece right onto my face.

Struggling to wipe the cake off my eyelid, I blinked to see twin figures holding pizza slices.

The movie wrapped up, leaving behind empty pizza boxes as Sia and I synchronized our yawns.

"I seriously need some sleep," Alaina announced, another yawn sneaking up on her.

"Totally," I chimed in with enthusiasm!

We cleaned up the mess of boxes and blankets scattered across the floor.

As I headed towards Alaina's room, I heard Raghav calling my name.

"Need something?" I asked.

"I've got something for you," he said.

"Uh, okay," I replied, surprised–after six years of knowing each other, this was the first time he'd ever given me a gift.

As I approached his bedroom door, he halted me.

Returning with a box that resembled a jewellery case, I was genuinely surprised–

"You really didn't need to," I murmured.

Lifting the lid, I discovered a pendant adorned with a star.

A note accompanied it, with a simple message–

"Now, go to your room. I'm exhausted."

"Thank you–" I began, but he cut me off.

"Yeah, yeah, bye now," he waved me off.

Oh ok.

-Dearest stary,

You shine the brightest.

****

SIA

Eighteen

I have written letters to many, thanking them for being there but this one is for me, the girl who didn't lose herself

Thank you, cause the truth is no matter the condition you were there, fighting. You lost battles and you found yourself in the failing nest at times but you stood up again.

You fought that voice that surrounded you, you tried but still wasn't appreciated and I know how painful that is. You live for pleasing people and it's hard to get back from that road, you try but still find yourself at point zero. You've lost friends, many in fact, you have lost yourself, maybe incomplete is that correct word. I don't want to feel this knot anymore. I don't want to feel pressured to achieve something, to be called worth it. Cause none of them have seen your battles. The ones you fought in the darkness of night, covering your mouth so that no one hears your screams. No one has seen the knife you held while they yelled. I am proud of you but sometimes I feel exhausted. There are days when you don't find a reason to get up and put all that energy into trying again, trying to win over people's hearts, trying to find your worth in others comments, trying to be like them, but somehow after all this you are still a nobody.

Looking at this drop of tear, which portrayed, unacceptance from the world.

SIA

Nineteen

As I walked out with 2 bags in my hand, I heard my phone buzzing. I handled the bags when I answered without looking and it was too late when I actually noticed who it was - Aanya.

The named saved as - 2/2/22 *heart emoji* -

the date when we met.

"hello" I started with a confusion face.

"You know, I couldn't believe you did this. But who am I kidding after everything what I can I even expect"

What?

"wait what!" I said with no clue where this was going.

"I knew it you will try to act dumb" I knew this was going to go bad.

"What are you even talking about!"

"You have no right talking about me and Kai"

"Yeah, so?" I replied, still clueless.

Kai? Oh right! We dated for a while, fun fact we broke up because of Aanya (NOT pointing any fingers).

I still remember.

"Hey! With all respect. I don't care."

"Good! Always remember that he broke up with you" she said.

"I remember and also I- "

"I never thought that you would talk behind my back" she attacked.

"Wait! Like back bitched!?"

"Yes, I have never in my life talked shit about you"

"Sorry but let me stop you right there. You have back bitched multiple time; I just never had the gut to confess it to you" I said, feeling a different level of strength in me.

"PLEASE!"

"Oh really, what about when you and Aarna practically screamed in your bus" I confessed.

"that's not bitching because that's my best friend"

What!

I practically laughed at that explanation.

"You on the other hand" she continued.

"Are telling people you and Kai"

"I think you are just thinking too high of yourself." I try to act as okay with conversation as I can, though I hate fight with her!

"You know what, I just think you are just totally obsessed with us and still haven't moved on"

I think that's when she got me.

But how do you move on from friendships.

She muted herself before saying it, and I couldn't help but smirk.

She was totally using my own trick against me.

It took me back to when she used to confront people, and I'd be right there next to her, whispering suggestions of comebacks, while she muted her phone call.

As we continued arguing or as she said "discussing" I couldn't help but feel like crumbling into a corner,

"I know with your Nani passing it must be hard". She didn't

"Don't! We both know you don't care so don't, don't bring her in this conversation!"

It actually felt disrespectful to even mention her.

As I continued defending myself from a corner in the mall beside the elevator,

I knew this is just useless, so in the respect that I had for every memory we had I softly said

"This is useless"

I called my car and leaped into it before busting into tears,

Even after this, my phone kept buzzing and with text and call of hers.

When I reached home,

I got this one notification before I decided to turn it off but this wasn't from Aanya but it was your Alaina.

It was one of her memes; I went forward and opened it but this wasn't one of her cute cat and dogs video but it said –

DON'T COMPLICATE LIFE:

Missing someone? – call

Wanna meet up? – invite

Wanna be understood? – explain

Love someone? – tell them

I don't know what but it seemed like one of those signs you know which are meant for you.

I picked up my phone. Wiping off my stars

And –

Calling ... 2/2/22 *heart emoji* -

"Hey. I can't destroy the year because of few months of misunderstanding, we can't fix this, so I decide not to destroy it. Take care and

Radhe Radhe"

"Radhe Radhe" I got this soft and full of love in return

After everything,

I promise – I am always there for you!

SIA

Twenty

As we continue practising,
Shara kept joining us and Aanya left.

We all noticed Shara's different approach towards everything. She especially got close to Raghav over the period of time. He even offered to practise with her to make up for the lost time. Not going to lie, I was pretty (extremely) jealous but not to worry I had it under control (I kept surprisingly and totally coincidently showed up to interrupt their alone time).

Only 2 weeks were left for the match and 1 weeks to the dance.

Everyone had a partner, except me.

Truly there is only one person I wanna go with.

Raghav, if it wasn't clear.

I sat beside Shara.

"Coming to the dance?"

"Not really sure!"

"Oh, you should join us"

"Us?'

"The usual- Alaina, me and ...Raghav"

For some reason she almost jumped to say yes as I finished my sentence.

as we hit the court, we sweat blood and hill.

I caught Raghav and planned to meet for the fun Friday.

We started this thing when Alaina lost her dog, coco.

First, Tony's ice cream.

Followed by the bookstore (where Raghav stared at both us form outside the store because food wasn't allowed inside and he takes his beauty time with his Belgian chocolate, 2 scoops)

And we finished the evening by going to the movies.

I texted Alaina about the same before I left.

****

“I wanna try something new this time” Alaina screams

“Good take, you must have got tired of eating toothpaste” I say

“It tastes nothing like toothpaste” it so does.

“Mint chocolate” Raghav proves.

We bust through the door of Tony’s; I am sure our laughter that sounds like screams got everyone’s attention once.

As soon as we all decided our order, Alaina and I ate it up quick enough to have a brain-freeze.

“Got your partner?”

“Not yet.”

So, Alaina not completely knows about my mega liking for Raghav.

“don’t you have to practise for the opening act?”

“I do but...”

“When is this duffer going to come in use” she said as she pointed at Raghav and my heart for sure agreed to it.

“He already has a lot going on with the championship” shut up Sia.

“Please, it’s just a dance” I love you, Alaina.

“I will ask him later” I am crazy nervous.

RAGHAV

Twenty One

"Wanna go to our place before" Alaina asked Sia, after the 2 hrs of torture of a film.

"Not today, I have prep for the dance"

"Oh wait! didn't you have something to ask Raghav" Alaina slyly hinted, signalling towards me with her eyes.

I raised my eyebrows as I looked at Sia.

"Umm, it's nothing. I can manage"

"What! No."

"Listen! She needs a dance partner for the formal dinner and you got to be it" Alaina said like I would do whatever she asks me.

I was going to say no but then I casted a glance at Sia. I knew that she wouldn't have asked me if she wasn't in desperate need and I had to help her so...

"I will think about it"

As I put a thought into it,

I wanted to say No immediately.

I am sure Sia could easily pull a guy.

Though after seeing her with Alaina,

anyone would run for their sanity

I texted Sia at

Raghav - Sure! Let's do it

Sia – thanks this means a lot. <3

SIA

Twenty Two

"I have decided whom to ask for the formal dinner" Shara said as she jumped to me.

"that's great!" that's when Raghav walked up to me,

"Raghav-" Shara got interrupted by Raghav's deep voice

"Let's go we have a lot to practice for the dance"

"Sure, give me a minute" I replied, as I turned to Shara.

"You said something?"

"No! just. You going with" she stopped as she turned to "Raghav"

“Oh yes! I couldn’t find anyone else, with all the practise and training, so I agree to tolerate his annoying sense of humour and he agreed to control his stupidity”

So not want happened, it was me to was asked to not be a yapper for a night and to not act as a headless freak. Though I strongly believe I never act that way

As I stood up to leave, I was called by the coach.

We were joined by the boy’s team today.

“Line up!”

We went over before he continued

“2 weeks! And we still need a captain for you all” he said pointing at us.

There were many in this team who were capable of the spot. Shara, especially her.

“Tomorrow, we decide. You’ll compete and we will see how you all work as a team.

We all know red and blue team is in shape but now it’s time to play as hawks!”

Shara shoulder bumped me. And we were dismissed.

I took Raghav to the studio where everything was set for the formal dinner.

“Wow! You all have turned this place around.” He said as we circled around.

I clapped my hands twice trying to mock him.

“Now stary. Let’s work on your moves.” I bend a little down and spread my legs, and clapped again.

“Stick to dancing because acting is for sure not for you” he said before he stepped towards me, my heart build castles in the air, before I dreamed a little too much

“let’s start” he screamed into my ear

Teaching this guy dance was worse than teaching a dog to play Jenga

With each step, he stumbled, his feet moving as if they were completely independent of his body. But despite the frustration, there was something endearing about the way he tried, his determination shining through his clumsy movements. even as he stumbled and laughed at his own missteps.

"Let's give it another shot," I encouraged, leading him back to the starting position. "Just relax and let the music guide you."

He nodded earnestly; his eyes locked onto mine as if seeking reassurance. As we began to move together, I couldn't help but notice the way his gaze softened, the tension melting away as he focused on the music and our connection.

As I guided him through the basic steps, our laughter filled the room. i couldn't help but smile as I watched him, his expression mixed with a hint of embarrassment whenever he missed a step.

As the music played softly in the background, I found myself lost in the moment, forgetting about everything else except the music and him.

And in that moment, as our hearts beat as one, I knew that I was falling for him all over again. But for now, all I could do was dance, letting the music carry us away into a world where nothing else mattered except the two of them.

SIA

Twenty Three

Ok. We lost!

WE LOST BIG TIME.

-7 to 23

And 4 parts of that were scored by Shara, 1 other by Zara and the rest by me.

I could see the boys grinning ear to ear. The urge to toss their stupid finger up their nose.

I looked at Raghav and though he was on the urge to bust out laughing but he still shoots me a calming look. As soon as I thought of not breaking his finger, he turned and high fived his team mate who was mocking our game play, those-

“Line up!” coach shut us up.

“Good job everyone!” he continued

“Except the girl’s team right!?” the same guy who mocked us said, it boiled my finger but Shara stopped me.

“Boys! You are dismissed” coach ordered, as the boys left still smirking, coach continued “you all did great”

One of us said “but we lost and look at the scores!”

“You have to look at the size of the them before judging and how long has it been since you all are playing but more importantly, we need captains. After seeing you all play it was clear only one knew the team well enough and also knew her way around the court” he did the classic dramatic pause.

It was like everybody knew it was me but we can’t be sure.

“It’s Shara” even she was taken back a little but then looked at me.

Don’t get me wrong, I was over the top but I can’t deny I was a little disappointed.

“As vice-captain, it’s going to be Sia” that’s great too.

****

"Vice-captain? You deserve to be the captain. You built the whole team. How could he?" Alaina screamed. I almost saw steam coming out her ears.

"I am sure he had a reason for his doing. He is pretty smart" Raghav said calmly.

"Smart! This sounds 'Stupid'." Alaina continued piercing my ears.

RAGHAV

Twenty Four

I stood there until they tried on a million looks, I mean how many types of dress can there be.

Though I grew up with a sister, I never saw this side of what they call 'girlhood'.

I always saw the – messy room, oversized t-shirt covered in paint splashes, hair tied into a bun.

I still remember when they got their first make up. Alaina got few million things there, though I wonder when does she even use it.

However, Sia got an eyelash comb with paint on it. She said that she didn't need anything else cause the - eyelash comb with paint on it, does all the work.

Even today she held one tube of it and her lip gloss against, Alaina's full blown make up kit.

We have been practicing franticly and I have no idea how she has been managing both for the last months. From the last few weeks, I climb up to bed and feel every bone burning form tiredness, bed seems to me as a pram, like dancing in the clouds.

Seeing Sia dance is like a view to heaven, like she is no longer control of her body. She feels every beat from something deep within.

I don't know, there's just something about her, something that pulls you in and won't let you go. It's like, you can't take your eyes off her, even if you wanted to. And when she looks at you, it's like she's seeing right into your soul.

being around her, watching her dance, it's like everything else just fades away. It's like she's the only thing that matters in that moment. And I can't help but feel like...like maybe there's something special there, something more than just watching her dance.

"How does this look?" Alaina asks with a whole lot of blue and black on her eyelids.

"Great" Sia looks into the mirror and opens the tube of lash comb and applying it all over her upper and lower lashes, though it looks risky the final product it magnificent.

“it’s crazy what difference mascara makes” Alaina says looking at Sia with huge eyes.

“Wanna practise a few more times before tomorrow?” I plead

“Sure!”

“Before that could explain how is this whole formal dinner going to work?” Alaina says.

Sia starts “It’s nothing big” Big? They have turned the whole auditorium into a disco ball.

Sia continues “They are just trying something new and to involve more people, we start with a dance, to represent the dance club and it continues with an open dance floor.”

SIA

Twenty Five

"Do I look fine?"

"You kidding? You look gorgeous!" this is what Alaina does. She makes you feel like the most beautiful creature on earth.

We climb into the elevator and I try to go through my extra straight hair, making sure it looks fluffy.

"Where's Raghav" I asked.

"We left home together; I came over here and he said he had something to do before the match" Alaina confessed. "He will be there!"

"Sure!"

The elevator doors opened and we stepped out and walked to the car.

Though I was crazy nervous for the performance I tried staying clam.

I texted Raghav,

Sia- Hey. Are you on our way, we have already left.

Raghav – yup

That's good.

We reached and caught up with everyone, I looked over to the music system and saw Zara handling it,

As the minutes passed, I felt more and more nervous,

When everyone called me to get staged, I texted Raghav who still hadn't reached nor was replying to my text.

I stood at the entrance with my arms crossed, with burning rage of a thousand suns.

I stood there waiting, clutching to my star around my neck.

I stood there waiting when everyone was performing,

And even when everyone hit the open dance floor.

When everyone seemed occupied, even Alaina, I sneaked off to my sanctuary for some warm hugs.

****

As I shooted few hoops in the silence I could feel and hear every thug.

While I released my anger into every hoop thinking I was alone.

“Shouldn’t you be at the dinner or” he took a pause “anywhere but here.”

I panicked by the voice and tired turned around in mid-air which resulted in falling on my back.

When I got upon my feet, coach got the ball and started to dribble it.

“What about a match?” coach asked

“Sure thing!” I replied

After 10 mins of intense dribbling, hooping and defence,

We sat and while trying to catch my breath, the air was heavy.

“Sir! If you don’t mind, could I ask something- “

“Is it about the captain’s position”

“Partially, it’s not that I was aiming for the captain’s position-” I was hesitant

“it’s that you feel like you deserve it, because its correct you do” he chugging to water.

He continued “You did deserve it, you built the team after all, but that’s not the only thing you see in a captain and its player. Shara might be more experienced than you but that doesn't mean she has the leadership like you but being so close to the championship, I couldn't let a feudal break out between the team, think about it!"

He is smart!

After all this, he stood up and I did too in respect and he left the court.

RAGHAV

Twenty Six

"Believe me or not. I wanted to be there!" I screamed trying to make my point.

"Yes? Good luck because Sia is neither picking up my phone nor responding to our texts" Alaina screams back.

I make my way to my room, slamming my door close.

I have to make it right but I really did want to be there.

The next day I tried talking to her during practice but all she did was ignore me.

When after 4 days she finally gave in,

"How could you just leave me there! Please! For the sake of our friendship. Don't Talk To Me"

As she finished screaming, I turned and left. I wasn't going to keep begging her!

I had my explanations but if she isn't interested then be it.

I focused on my practice while she did on hers.

Our match went down first, and then it was their turn.

Sia didn't hit the court during their first game, but honestly, I couldn't be bothered with the why. Anyway, they had their ups and downs, winning some, losing some. But when it came to the crunch on the fifth day - win or wave goodbye to the competition.

The tension was thick enough to slice with a butter knife, but then things took a turn. Sia was MIA, nowhere to be seen. She disappeared for a whole hour. When I heard she was missing, I dashed around searching everywhere. Panic started creeping in like a slow fog. I tore through, checking every nook.

While all this, Shara stood there screaming "Stop all this, we can play without her"

I knew they could "Sure! You all can", everyone looked my way "but you all can't win without her."

I knew everyone agreed with me but it was almost time but,

Really! Sia always supported Shara and she doesn't seem sightly bothered.

Then, just when despair was about to settle in for good, I caught a faint sound, like someone crying. Following it like a beacon, I ended up at the dance studio. Sneaking in, I found her, curled up tight, tears streaming down her face.

My heart twisted seeing her like that, all alone and upset. Without a second thought, I went to her, offering whatever comfort I could muster. It didn't matter why she was there or what had happened. All that mattered was that she wasn't alone anymore.

I sat down beside her, not saying a word. Sometimes, you don't need words, you just need someone to be there.

Eventually, she looked up at me, her eyes all puffy. Without a word, I reached out my hand. And in that moment, she grabbed onto it, like she was holding onto hope.

We were in this mess together...

Before it was too late, I informed everyone about her.

Though I knew I had to make it fast, I didn't wish to rush in that moment.

I explained how I got a call from Shara that night, crying with everything she had. I couldn't help it but go to her, she cried about how these were her first match after his dad's passing and she is scared to disappoint him and my phone died so I could neither inform Sia nor could keep up with time and when I was about to leave, Shara told me she liked me.

Though I didn't feel the same, it was quite messy and I got stuck.

"I understand!" Sia spoke in a whisper "remember calling Nani before every match. It's scary for me too. It's hard not hearing that laugh. I miss calling her sexy" she chuckled, I could see it in her eyes, she could she her here. She at least pretended of her presence.

"The team needs you" I stood up and offered a hand to her "For Nani"

She smiled through her tears and stood up and nodded.

She shined as always. She was the best on court.

However, they lost but I could see her smiling bigger than ever and happy.

As the match was over, she came up to me and surrounded me into a hug.

"I have something for you" she said,

"So do I"

We both rushed to our backpack and pulled our surprises for each other.

I pulled out my manuscript, which was in fact dedicated to her and she pulled out a letter with a broken seal.

Mine had "written hearts" written over it and hers had 'love' written all over it.

We couldn't stop smiling as we handed it over to each other.

"*I want to gaze into your eyes until the moon drowns below those ocean waves. Until each whisper is told by the rain. Until you bring eternity with your touch ....* TO ME" she read out, her cheeks tinted rosy.

Seeing her, I wish I could tell her how all this is for her. How she makes me feel all these feelings which I expressed in here.

And I noticed how Sia had described this piece of envelope before "Is this Nani's letter?" I blurted out

"Yes! She took many years to figure out love but I don't want to sit on my death bed wondering what love feels like, want to figure it out together" she said, I could she her blushing from the corner of my eyes.

She was beautiful, in that moment I struggled to confess that my book what about her!

As she glanced down, embarrassed for what it showed. I approached for Nani's clutcher on the corner of her jersey's and clutched it onto my hair "I am here! For as long as you need me" I declared.

Her huge eyes met mine, they held a universe of emotions.

Understanding me like no one ever did.

In moments like this, her eyes sparkled like sunlight dancing on water, infectious laughter that lit up her entire face.

For that moment and that moment only, my life seemed perfect.

She eyes held depth, as if she held the answers to life's greatest mysteries

Mysteries like "love".

Twenty Seven

It's tough when people part ways, especially when neither of you were prepared for it. Sometimes, facing pain becomes a habit, even though wounds eventually heal. Yet, despite the healing, it's like stocking up on concealer to mask the scars. Looking at your reflection, you might feel like a stranger in your own skin. And though others may have labeled you as fake, now it's like an itch deep within your bones, a discomfort with your own identity. But remember, beneath the layers, your true self shines through, resilient and worthy of love and acceptance.

THE END